Teddy's
First Christmas

Teddy's
First Christmas

AMANDA DAVIDSON

FONTANA
PICTURE LIONS

For Andrew

First published in Great Britain 1982 by William Collins Sons & Co Lt
First published in Picture Lions 1985
by William Collins Sons & Co Ltd
8 Grafton Street, London W1 X 3LA
© Text and illustrations Amanda Davidson 1982
Printed in Great Britain
by William Collins Sons & Co Ltd, Glasgow

It is Christmas Eve. Everyone is asleep.

Look at the presents piled under the tree.

Look at the big red box with the ribbon on top.

There's somebody inside. . . .

It's Teddy!

Hello Teddy.

"What's that?" says Teddy.

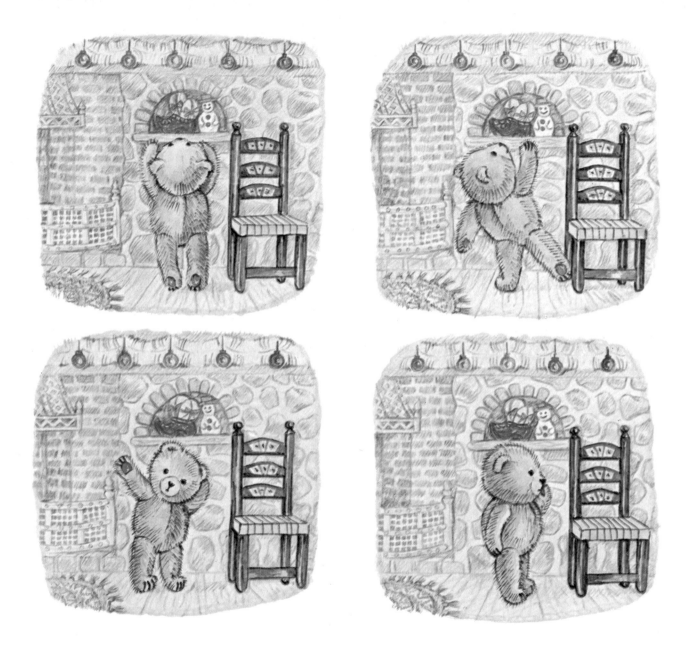

"It's very hard to reach."

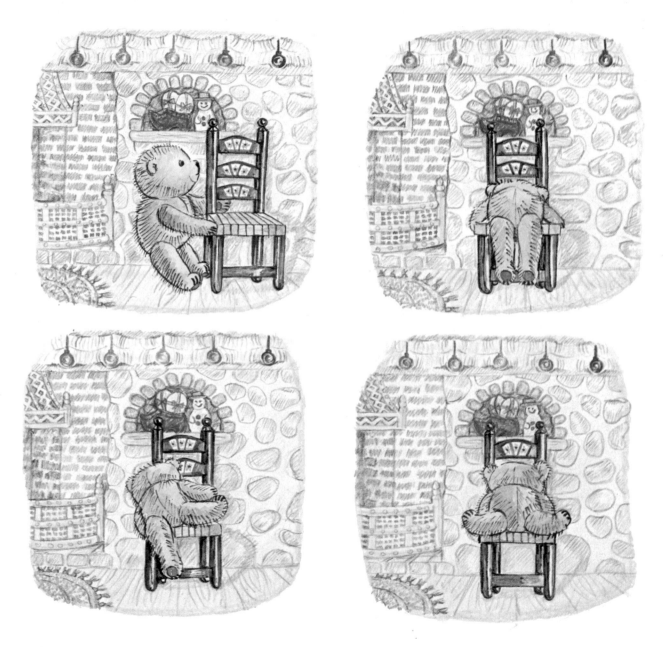

"What shall I do?"

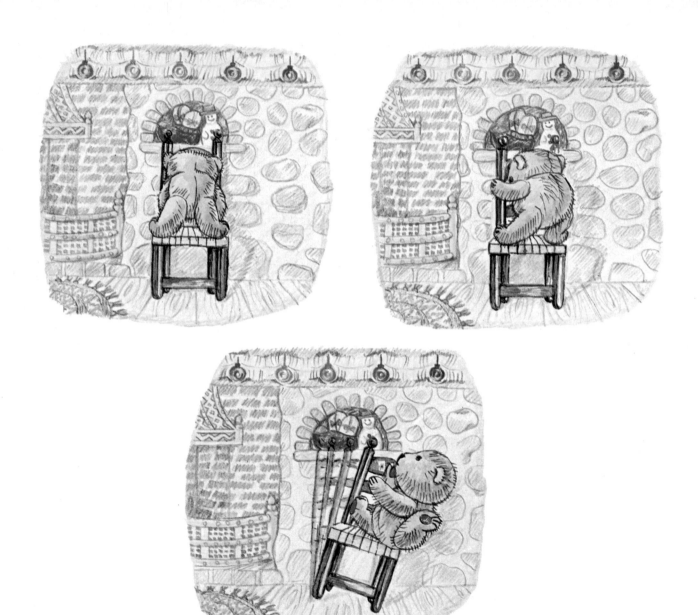

Be **careful**, Teddy.

Oh dear! Up you get.

"Who's that?" says Teddy.

"I'd like to talk to her."

Be **careful**, Teddy.

Oh dear! Up you get.

"And what's this?" says Teddy.

"I'll pull it and see."

Pull, pull, and . . .

up in the air . . . and . . .

back in the box,

ready for Christmas morning!

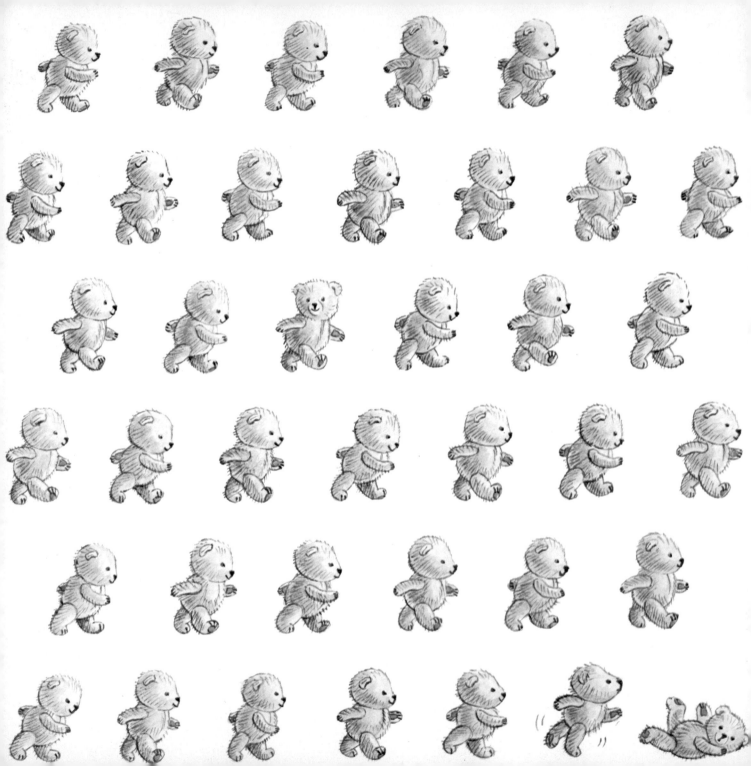